Susan's Journey

Step Through the Wardrobe

Susan's Journey
Step Through the Wardrobe

Adapted by Alison Sage

HarperCollins*Publishers*

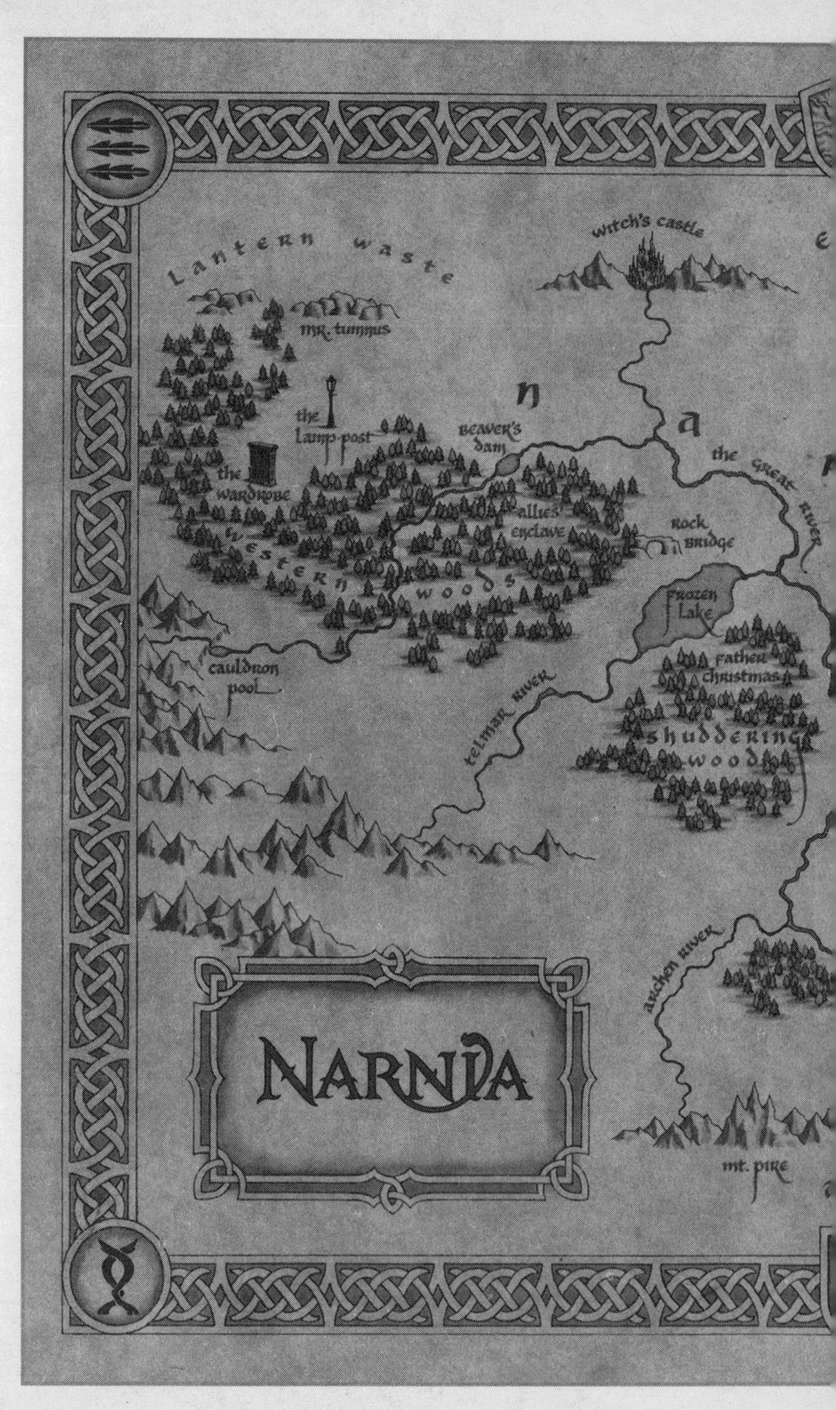

Lantern waste
witch's castle
mr. tumnus
the lamp-post
beaver's dam
the wardrobe
allies' enclave
rock bridge
the great river
western woods
frozen lake
cauldron pool
father christmas
telmar river
shuddering wood
archen river
NARNIA
mt. pire

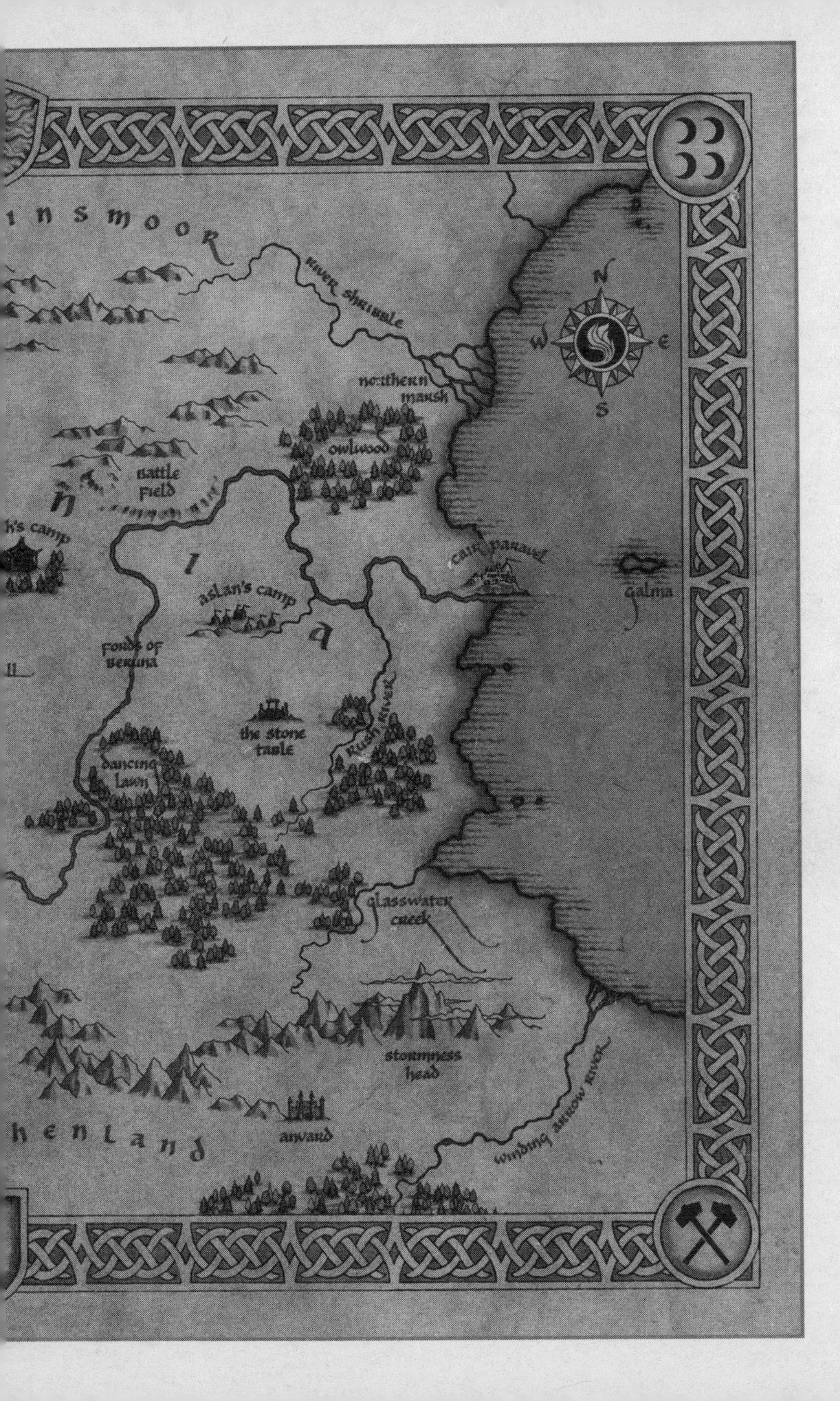

insmoor
river shribble
northern marsh
owlwood
battle field
k's camp
aslan's camp
fords of beruna
the stone table
Rush River
dancing lawn
cair paravel
Galma
N
S
E
W
glasswater creek
stormness head
anvard
henland
winding arrow river

NARNIA®

Susan's Journey: *Step Through the Wardrobe*
 For information address HarperCollins Children's Books, a division of HarperCollins Publishers, 1350 Avenue of the Americas, New York, NY 10019.
www.narnia.com

Library of Congress catalog card number: 2005931866
ISBN-10: 0-06-085237-2 (pbk.) — ISBN-13: 978-0-06-085237-5 (pbk.)
ISBN-10: 0-06-085238-0 (trade bdg.) — ISBN-13: 978-0-06-085238-2 (trade bdg.)

❖

Contents

Chapter One

Leaving Home

The room was pitch black. That meant the blackout was safely in place. *Good,* thought Susan as she lay in the darkness. At least no German planes could see their house. It was 1941 and the bombs fell almost every night over London. Every morning there were stories of houses gutted, families destroyed. Sometimes these things happened to people she knew. Susan didn't talk about it much because it upset their mother, especially now that Father was away in the air force.

Susan didn't like the War at all, and the way nothing was straightforward and under control. She felt helpless. Tomorrow, she and her brothers, Peter and Edmund, and her little sister, Lucy, were being evacuated from the dangerous city to stay with Professor Kirke in the safety of the countryside. Like thousands of other children, they were going to a place they didn't know, all by themselves. Susan felt tears rising and she choked them back. Mother had explained to her how important it was to keep cheerful so that the younger ones wouldn't be afraid. Mother trusted her to keep the family together. Peter was the oldest, but Susan knew that a lot of the responsibility rested on her shoulders. Edmund was impulsive, and little Lucy could be very determined.

Suddenly, Susan felt the house shake. The bombs were dropping again. She ran downstairs and out to the bomb shelter at the bottom of the garden. Edmund was being silly and running back into the house. Soon he emerged with a photo of their father and charged into the shelter. "Idiot!" shouted Peter. But Susan thought Edmund had been brave.

In the morning, there was a frenzied rush as the children got their things together. Mother hugged Susan good-bye, and then they were on the train and pulling out of the station.

Susan didn't know what she had expected, but nothing had prepared her for the huge rambling old house, or for the Professor's disagreeable housekeeper, Mrs. Macready. Mrs. Macready seemed to have been born mean.

"There shall be no shouting or running," she snapped. "And above all, there shall be no disturbing of the Professor."

But Susan persevered. She tried to be cheerful.

She tried to get the others to see how important it was to keep doing normal things, like going to bed on time and brushing their teeth.

The next day, it was pouring rain and Susan's heart sank. There could be no exploring outside, and indoors everything was forbidden. It would be just like Edmund to break something and get them all into trouble. He was already being especially nasty, teasing little Lucy. Susan thought it would be a good idea if they all played a dictionary quiz. Perhaps it would stop Edmund from picking on Lucy. But Lucy said she wanted to play hide-and-seek. Edmund sneered at Lucy and told her hide-and-seek was only for little kids. Sometimes Susan didn't understand her younger brother at all. He could be a complete twerp.

In the end, Susan was glad that Peter let Lucy have her way, although she knew that he would

never have given in to Edmund like that—or her for that matter. Anything would be better than aimlessly wandering around that huge, dark house, arguing.

Peter started counting. "One, two, three . . ."

Susan had already discovered a good place to hide. Peter would never find her in the old window seat. This might be fun after all. Just as she was lowering herself into it, Lucy ran toward her. Frantically, Lucy dived off to find somewhere else.

"Forty-one, forty-two, forty-three . . ." chanted Peter.

Susan could hear Edmund and Lucy arguing about who was going to hide behind the velvet curtain.

"Eighty-nine, ninety . . ."

Edmund won. Susan knew he would. She heard Lucy dash off again.

"Ninety-nine, one hundred. Ready or not, here I come!"

Then something truly odd happened. The wardrobe door creaked open and Lucy shouted, "It's all right! I'm back!"

Back from where? What was happening?

Susan heard the angry, irritable voices of her brothers. She climbed out of her hiding place.

"Does this mean I win?" she asked, half-joking.

"Lucy doesn't want to play anymore," said Peter.

"I *was* playing," cried Lucy. "I was hiding in the wardrobe and next thing I was in a wood and I met a Faun named Mr. Tumnus . . ."

Susan looked at Peter anxiously. Was Lucy playing some kind of make-believe game? It didn't sound like a game. She was too upset, too bewildered. There was only one thing to do. Susan pulled back the coats in the big, old wardrobe. "Lucy, the only wood in here is the back of the wardrobe," she said firmly.

The next few hours were a blur of bad temper and ever-deepening mystery. Lucy insisted tearfully that she had been gone for hours in a strange country called Narnia, where it was always winter and never Christmas, and that she'd had tea with a Faun named Mr. Tumnus. How could she? She had only been gone for a couple of seconds. But she kept sobbing that it was true. Edmund wouldn't stop teasing her until Peter got furious with him and started telling them all what to do. It was unbearable and Susan could hardly wait to go to bed. Perhaps the next day would be better. It must be the rain that was making them all so mean to each other.

But it wasn't.

That night, Susan woke up to find that Lucy was gone! Scared, she jumped out of bed and ran to the boys' room. There was her sister, sitting on Peter's bed, babbling on about her mysterious snow-country again! She must have been dreaming. Only this time, she seemed to think that she had been there with Edmund. And this was the strange part: Why should she tell such a stupid lie? Edmund, of course, said she was just pretending . . . but alarm bells were ringing for Susan. If anyone told a lie, it was usually Edmund. Why would Lucy say something that was so obviously not true? It didn't make sense.

All the racket brought Mrs. Macready out in a foul temper, and then the Professor. Susan was almost glad to see him. He seemed like a sensible grown-up, and she and Peter explained everything to him.

But later that night, Susan went to bed in a troubled state of mind. The Professor's logical, ordered mind had come up with some very *illogical* conclusions. He seemed to suggest that this Narnia place really existed!

"If Lucy isn't lying, and if she's not crazy, then

logically, we must assume she's telling the truth."

But a forest at the back of a wardrobe? It was impossible.

The next day, the weather was better, but their tempers weren't. Susan persuaded her brothers to play cricket. Although the boys usually loved any ball game, today they did nothing but argue. In the end, Edmund deliberately whacked Peter's ball as wildly as he could, and Susan watched in horror as it crashed straight through the library window.

"Well done, Ed," said Peter, bitterly.

"You bowled it," sulked Edmund.

They all ran upstairs to look at the damage. Then they heard the familiar heavy footsteps of Mrs. Macready, the housekeeper.

"The Macready!" cried Susan in a panic as all four children ran out of the library.

They slipped into the room with Lucy's old

wardrobe. But Mrs. Macready seemed to have a sixth sense about where they were hiding. The footsteps stopped just outside the room.

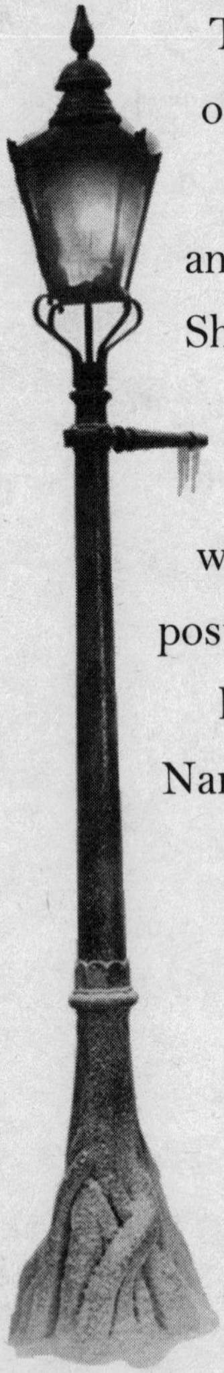

There was nothing to do but dive into the old wardrobe.

Susan felt blindly through the fur coats and her fingers touched . . . something cold. She stumbled forward, amazed. Instead of the solid, comforting back of the wardrobe, there was a silent, snowy wood shining in the light of an old lamp-post.

It was impossible. . . . Unless . . . Was this Narnia?

Chapter Two

Step Through the Wardrobe

Susan stared. She couldn't quite take everything in. Was this Lucy's strange country? But that was impossible! They were at the back of a wardrobe, for goodness sake! And was that a lamppost? What was a lamppost doing in a forest? It couldn't be real. But little snowflakes were settling on her bare hand and—real or not—she could feel a damp patch where the snow was melting on her sleeve.

She took a step forward into the whirling flakes.

"Peter?" She whispered uncertainly.

But Peter was looking at Lucy with new respect. She ran to them, grinning with excitement, her hair freckled with snow.

"I don't suppose saying we're sorry would quite cover it," said Peter.

"You're right." Lucy giggled. "It wouldn't, but *this* would," and she scooped up a handful of powdery snow and threw it at him.

Some of the snow exploded on Susan. She automatically bent down and threw a cloud of icy crystals back at her sister. Soon there was a pitched battle. Everyone was screaming with laughter as the soft snow flew in their faces and down their collars. Everyone except Edmund. He looked guilty and uncomfortable, as if he wasn't enjoying himself. Someone—perhaps it was Peter—threw a snowball at him and hit him in the face. He yelled out angrily to stop it. Suddenly, everyone stopped.

All at once, things became clear in Susan's mind. So *that* was why Edmund had been so nasty to Lucy! He really *had* been to this Narnia place before. How mean of him! He had deliberately made Lucy look silly because he wanted to keep the secret for himself! But when had he come? And why did he want to keep it a secret? It didn't make sense. Suddenly, Susan felt scared. Everything was just too strange, too bizarre. Normal, ordinary children like them didn't belong here.

"Maybe we should go back," she said uncomfortably.

But Peter wasn't listening to her.

"I think Lucy should decide," he said.

It was not in Lucy's nature to bear a grudge, and she was brimming with happiness at finding Narnia again.

"I want you to meet Mr. Tumnus," she said excitedly.

Her enthusiasm was infectious and Susan started to think that maybe she would like to have tea with a Faun. They set off with Lucy delightedly leading the way.

But when Lucy suddenly stopped, all Susan could do was stare. Something was very wrong with the little stone house in front of her. The door was wrenched off its hinges, and there were signs of a desperate struggle.

Lucy looked around at the damaged house. "Who would do something like this?" she asked.

The walls were blackened with smoke and

everything was smashed and tipped on the floor. Susan's heart lurched. This was bad, very bad. In a quiet voice, Peter read out a notice that had been pinned to the floor.

"The Faun Tumnus is hereby charged
with High Treason against her
Imperial Majesty Jadis,
Queen of Narnia,
for comforting her enemies
and fraternizing with Humans.
Signed, Maugrim,
Captain of the Secret Police.
Long live the Queen."

Susan was horrified. If this could happen to the Faun, what would happen to *them*? They didn't even live there. They had to go. Mother would want all of them safely back through

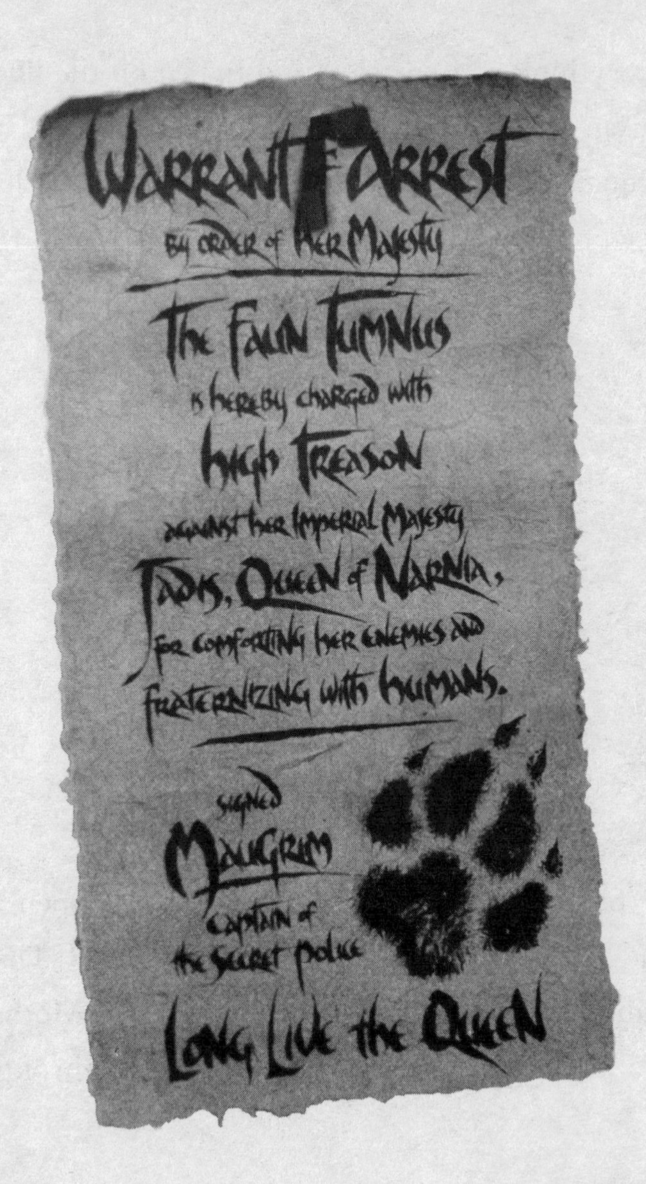

WARRANT OF ARREST

BY ORDER OF HER MAJESTY

THE FAUN TUMNUS

IS HEREBY CHARGED WITH

HIGH TREASON

AGAINST HER IMPERIAL MAJESTY

JADIS, QUEEN OF NARNIA,

FOR COMFORTING HER ENEMIES AND

FRATERNIZING WITH HUMANS.

SIGNED

MAUGRIM

CAPTAIN OF

THE SECRET POLICE

LONG LIVE THE QUEEN

the wardrobe, and if Peter wouldn't do anything, it was up to her to show some common sense.

"All right, now we really should go back," she said firmly.

But Lucy was babbling on to Peter about this Mr. Tumnus.

"I'm the Human! She must have found out he helped me," Lucy said. But how could it be her fault? She was only a little girl. Why should anyone be punished for giving Lucy tea?

"Maybe we could call the police," suggested Peter.

"These *are* the police," responded Susan.

"Don't worry, Lu," said Peter. "We'll think of something."

"Why?" demanded Edmund. "I mean, he's a criminal." Edmund gestured to the warrant and continued, "And how do we even know that the Queen's not in the right?"

This sounded odd to Susan. How could her brother be so unfair?

All of a sudden, Susan heard a loud, "Pssst!" She turned around to see a large Beaver beckoning to them. It had such a stern look in its eyes that she bit back the impulse to shout that talking Beavers were not possible. Perhaps she was dreaming. There was no point in arguing with a dream.

But the Beaver did not sound like a dream. He was holding Lucy's handkerchief and he told them fiercely that they were being watched, so they had better follow him to his dam. Lucy, of course, trotted after him immediately, and Peter followed her. Susan dared not split up the family, so she stumbled after them through the snow, with Edmund lagging behind.

The Beaver's dam was huge, and Susan had to admit that she was glad to scramble into its comforting warmth. It smelled of nice things to eat and felt safe, somehow. Mrs. Beaver welcomed them with a kind smile on her whiskery face.

"Come inside and we'll see if we can't get you some food," she said, heaping fresh fish on their plates.

"Isn't there anything we can do to help Mr. Tumnus?" asked Peter.

But Susan couldn't help noticing that the Beavers did not look very hopeful.

"They have taken him to the Witch's house," said Mr. Beaver soberly. "And there's few who go through those gates who ever come out again."

Susan began to feel very uncomfortable.

Then something strange happened. Mrs. Beaver started talking about someone named Aslan, and how he was the true King of Narnia and how he would help them to find Mr. Tumnus. And just hearing his name made Susan feel better. Perhaps it was because she had been hungry and they had just eaten a good meal, but this Aslan seemed like someone who you could trust, who would take away all the strange, scary feelings she had when things weren't clear and under control.

"He's waiting for you at the Stone Table," said Mr. Beaver.

Why should this Aslan wait for them, Susan

wondered. They were going straight back to the Professor's house. Surely these Beavers realized that. . . . ?

"You've never heard of Aslan?" continued Mr. Beaver, amazed. (As if they could! They had only just arrived!) "But there is a prophecy!" And he repeated a funny little verse, all about two boys and two girls who would lead an army with Aslan against the White Witch and bring peace to Narnia.

Susan was now struggling to make sense of it all. These Beavers must have made a mistake. They couldn't mean them. They were just four children from London and they were escaping a war, not fighting one! It was all really out of control. Before, it had just been a slightly peculiar dream, but this was getting dangerous. She had to do something.

Susan stood up quickly. "Thank you for your hospitality and everything," she said, staring

hard at Peter, "but we really have to go."

Mr. Beaver and Lucy started to protest but, to Susan's relief, Peter got to his feet.

"I'm sorry, but it's time the four of us were getting home," he agreed.

The three of them looked at Edmund's chair. It was empty!

Susan felt a lump in her throat. Where was her brother? What had Edmund done that first time in Narnia? They had never really asked him. Mr. Beaver's eyes were wide and upset.

"Has Edmund ever been to Narnia before?" asked Mr. Beaver.

The children ran out into the snow. In the distance, they could see Edmund running toward two hills and on the top of a cliff between them was a dark, gloomy-looking castle. Peter and Susan ran after Edmund, calling for him to come back.

"You're playing into her hands!" cried Mr. Beaver desperately.

"We can't let him go," explained Susan.

"He's the bait," replied Mr. Beaver. "The Witch wants all four of you! To stop the prophecy from coming true. . . . *To kill you!*"

Chapter Three

On the Run

Susan had never felt as helpless in her life as she did when she watched Edmund climb the cliff towards the gaunt, shadowy castle.

Couldn't he see that they mustn't split up? Now none of them could go home. They had to stay and get him back. Susan wasn't sure she liked the Beavers, but they did seem to be telling the truth. This White Witch, whatever Edmund thought, was clearly very dangerous. Who knows what she could do to him?

Edmund hauled himself to the top and walked through a huge dark doorway without even a backward glance. The gates clanged behind him. Tears of rage and desperation came into Susan's eyes.

"This is all your fault!" she cried. "None of this would have happened if you'd listened to me in the first place!"

Peter looked at her angrily, "Oh, so you knew this would happen?"

Lucy jumped in crying, "Stop it!"

Mr. Beaver watched them arguing with sad dark eyes.

"Only Aslan can help your brother now," he said.

"Fine," said Peter. "Then take us to him."

They tumbled into the dam where Mrs.

Beaver had already started to pack some food. Susan felt a glow of sympathy and she began to help put things in a basket. It was a relief to do something practical.

"Do you think we'll need jam?" asked Susan.

Suddenly there was a horrible bloodcurdling howl from just outside the dam. It sounded like the cry of a pack of hunting Wolves.

"Only if the Witch serves toast," Peter replied.

No one stopped to argue. They tumbled after Mr. Beaver as he yanked open a cupboard door and disappeared down a tunnel, slamming the door shut as they went.

It was dark and narrow in the tunnel, and full of tree roots.

"A Badger friend dug this," explained Mr.

Beaver. "It comes up near his place."

"Shhh!" cried Lucy. "They're in the tunnel!"

Mr. Beaver began scrabbling about in the roots above their heads. Soon they could see a dark patch of sky as he scrambled out and everyone followed as fast as they could.

Susan gave a sigh of relief. It was good to

breathe the cold frosty air again, and there in front of them was a little village lying peacefully in the moonlight. Then she realized with a shock that something was very wrong. Otters, Squirrels, and Rabbits seemed to be playing and going about their business. Except that they weren't. They were frozen and still. Every one had been turned to stone by the White Witch.

Later that night during a brief rest, they sat around the fire discussing what to do next.

Mrs. Beaver said nothing, but Susan saw how worried she looked.

This journey was going to be risky. If only they could stop pretending to be Kings and Queens and heroes. If only Edmund hadn't run away! But Peter was almost as bad. He seemed to be caught up in this war and dangerous stuff and Susan had a secret fear that he *wanted* to be a hero and lead an army against the White Witch.

He had always made a fuss over little Lucy, but he used to talk to her, Susan, about sensible things. Now he seemed to pay attention to Lucy all the time.

If only he had listened to me right at the beginning, none of this would have happened, Susan thought angrily. They would be safe at home in their beds, with nothing more scary to look forward to than Mrs. Macready.

The next day didn't bring any answers, either. At one point, they stood on a rock bridge and Narnia spread out before for them glittering endlessly white in the sunshine.

"Aslan's camp should be near the Stone Table," said Mr. Beaver cheerfully. "Just across the Great River."

He pointed many miles in the distance to a faint hill with a stone on the top.

"Well, there's a bright side to everything," grumbled Susan. But she knew there wasn't any choice. Behind them were the Wolves and the White Witch.

Hour after hour they plodded over the vast frozen lake, aware that they were visible for miles around like five ants on a white tablecloth.

"Hurry up! Run! Run!" The Beavers galloped easily over the ice and they kept nagging the children to hurry.

"Behind you, it's her!" shrieked Mrs. Beaver.

Susan risked a glance over her shoulder and wished she hadn't. In the distance, she could clearly see plumes of flurrying snow. Behind them emerged a speeding sleigh with a tall figure holding the reins. It was catching up fast.

Susan tried to run but her exhausted legs wouldn't hold her up, and she slipped and slithered in her panic. She flung herself desperately after the others as they dashed into the shelter of some rocks.

"Inside! Dive! Dive!" ordered Mr. Beaver and they dived into a narrow hole.

Trembling, Susan could hear the sleigh bells growing louder.

She's going to find us! she thought. *And then, will she turn us all into stone?*

There was a quiet hiss of runners and the sleigh stopped.

A tall shadow passed over the mouth of the hole. They waited for what seemed like hours, but it could only have been a few minutes. Then Peter said bravely, "I suppose I'll go look."

"No, you are worth nothing to Narnia dead," said Mr. Beaver. Susan couldn't help seeing the relief in Peter's eyes as the old Beaver slipped out of the hole. But poor Mrs. Beaver was clearly very upset and frightened, and Susan slipped her hand into Mrs. Beaver's and gave it a squeeze. It was the only thing she could do.

Suddenly, they heard laughter. It was Mr. Beaver and his whiskery face filled the entrance to the hole.

"Come out! There's someone here to see you!" he grinned.

Susan cautiously poked her head out of the hole and stopped. There in front of her was a tall man in a red robe and a great white beard. He had a sword at his hip, but otherwise he looked just like—surely not! Lucy had already run up to him crying, "Merry Christmas, sir."

Father Christmas looked down at them and smiled. "It certainly is, Lucy," agreed Father Christmas. "Now that you've arrived."

Father Christmas laughed a rich, warm sound

that made them all feel comfortable and safe.

"But I thought there was no Christmas in Narnia," said Susan.

"Not for a long time. But the hope you have brought us, your Majesties, is finally weakening the Witch's magic. Still . . ." Father Christmas reached into his sack and pulled out some presents. "You could probably use these."

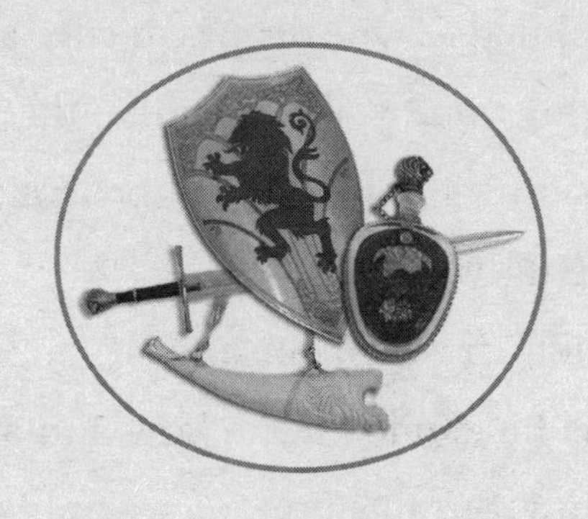

Chapter Four

A Visit from Father Christmas

Susan couldn't help feeling a bubble of excitement inside her. Presents . . . She forgot how scared she had been only a few moments earlier and watched eagerly as Father Christmas bent down to Lucy and gave her a shining jeweled vial. "The juice of the fireflower," said Father Christmas quietly. "One drop will cure any injury. And though I hope you never have to use it . . ." Father Christmas pulled a dagger from his sack. "Battles are ugly."

And then it was Susan's turn. She felt awkward as he handed her a bow and a quiver of arrows. "Now, Susan," he said warmly. "Trust in this bow and it will not easily miss."

"What happened to 'Battles are ugly'?" said Susan before she could stop herself.

Father Christmas laughed. "And though you don't seem to have a problem making yourself heard . . ." He gave her a beautiful little carved horn. "Blow this and wherever you are, help will come."

"Thanks," said Susan, for once at a loss for words.

Father Christmas turned to Peter and gave him a wonderful sword. It looked extremely

sharp and was covered in strange writing. He was given a shield, too, with a red lion on it.

"Thank you," said Peter, awed as he examined his new weapon.

Then Father Christmas climbed into his sleigh, cracked the reins and the eight snowy reindeer pulled the sleigh smoothly off across the ice.

Everyone was so excited. Nothing that Mr. Beaver said could get them to move until they had each admired everything. Their mood had lifted since meeting Father Christmas and even the air seemed warmer and smelled sweeter than before.

This cheerful optimism came to a sudden end when they reached the river. Winter was losing its grip: The ice was melting and the river was no longer safe to travel across. Huge cracks were running along its surface, and dark green water was leaking out. Every so often a sharp explosion like a rifle shot would signal that another massive lump of ice was breaking off. Above the river was a frozen waterfall, but that, too, was collapsing in a million splinters of ice.

"Our shortcut is melting," cried Susan as the full danger of the situation came home to them all. But Peter was determined to push on, "We need to cross now!"

"Will you think about this for a minute?" Susan was once again the voice of caution.

A mournful howl cut through the air, followed by another, even closer.

"We don't *have* a minute," said Peter.

He took one step onto the swaying ice.

"Maybe I should go first," said Mr. Beaver, and the ice groaned ominously as they all stepped onto it. Susan wavered in an agony of indecision.

"If Mum knew what you were doing," she said bitterly to Peter.

"Mum's not here," said Peter shortly, and as he spoke, the ice behind them cracked in two. Now

they couldn't get back even if they wanted to.

Painfully, they slithered forward across the shivering, crunching ice, and Susan found it hard to keep her balance. Once she fell heavily on Mrs. Beaver's tail and it hurt a lot, but Peter just shrugged in exasperation.

Then a lump of ice smashed down and they all looked up, startled. Silhouetted against the frozen waterfall above them, Susan could see the shapes of two huge Wolves.

Susan saw Peter draw his sword and push Lucy behind him. The Wolves, sensing that the children were trapped, leapt down in front of them. As if by a signal, one Wolf slipped sideways to menace Mr. Beaver, but the bigger Wolf trotted up to Peter.

"Put that down, boy," he said pleasantly, "someone could get hurt."

The second Wolf nipped viciously at Mr. Beaver and Susan could see that Peter didn't know what to do.

Peter's sword wavered and the Wolf began again.

"Leave now while you can, and your brother leaves with you."

This was the chance Susan had been waiting for. If only Peter would listen to this creature, they might still save Edmund and get away.

"Stop, Peter. Maybe we should listen to him!" she shouted.

"Smart girl!" snarled the Wolf softly.

"Look, just because some guy in a red suit gives you a sword it doesn't make you a hero! Just drop it!"

"No! Peter!" cried old Mr. Beaver painfully as the second Wolf gripped him with razor teeth. "Narnia needs you!"

Peter's sword wavered again. He obviously couldn't make up his mind. Susan was in agony. Why didn't he save them while he could?

"What will it be, Son of Adam!" Maugrim grinned maliciously. "I won't wait forever and neither will the river."

Just at that moment, a massive ice chunk crashed down from the waterfall and the river's surface of ice began shaking wildly as new cracks shot out in all directions. Susan felt herself falling, and heard Peter scream, "Hold on to me!" She managed to grab onto his coat and reach out for Lucy. She saw Peter, with a wild expression

on his face, lift up his sword and stab it down into the ice. She saw Maugrim's yellow eyes widen in astonished fury as the ice split.

Then the waterfall collapsed and a huge wave hit their little ice island and whirled them downstream in a violent torrent. Beavers, Wolves, ice—everything tossed like rags in a furious raging surge.

Susan blacked out. When she came to, her fingers were clamped onto Peter's coat and she had her other arm around Lucy's neck.

Another wave of ice-cold water struck them, and for a few moments they were all choking and spluttering.

Susan rubbed her eyes and peered into the broken ice floes that bobbed past them, looking for a piece of wood they could use as an oar. Then she spotted something dark floating in the water—except that it couldn't be floating because it was coming toward them against the current. It was swimming . . . it was Mr. Beaver! And there was Mrs. Beaver behind him!

Susan grinned with relief and in a few moments, the Beavers were grasping the ice with their strong white teeth and pushing them slowly but surely to the bank.

It was then that Susan saw Peter clutching Lucy's empty coat.

"Nooo . . ." she whispered.

Suddenly, someone began coughing nearby. Susan sighed with relief as Lucy staggered up the bank.

"Has anyone seen my coat?"

"Don't worry, love," piped Mrs. Beaver. "Looks like you won't be needing it where you're going."

Everyone was staring, but not at her. A little

tree, which had been cold and white when they had arrived on the bank, had quietly released little brown buds, then bright, juicy leaves and now, without warning, it had burst into full bloom. Beautiful sweet blossoms drifted slowly to earth.

The sight of the spring woods bursting out all around gave them new heart and Susan found she was smiling as they struggled up the last hill.

Everyone was quiet as they approached the

crest of the hill. But where was Aslan? After that terrible journey, why wasn't he there to welcome them?

Then Lucy peered over the side of the hill. There below them on the plain was a huge army. So it *was* true! There really was going to be a battle!

Chapter Five

Aslan's Camp

Susan felt like she was in a dream, walking down the hill into that great encampment. Everywhere she looked there were creatures she had only seen in storybooks—Centaurs, Nymphs, water spirits and strange animals she could never even have imagined. All of them treated the four children with the greatest respect.

Now I know I'm dreaming, thought Susan to herself. *I'm Susan Pevensie from Finchley, tired, filthy, dirty and my hair hasn't been combed for days. And these creatures are behaving as if I'm royalty!*

"What's going on?" Susan asked. "Why are they all staring at us?"

"Maybe they think you look funny," offered Lucy.

Outside Aslan's tent, Susan could see Peter was nervous.

"We . . . have come to see . . . Aslan," said Peter bravely.

Susan was astonished as all the creatures knelt before them.

Then she saw a huge golden paw move out from under the tent flap. And suddenly there was Aslan, a great golden Lion shining in the sunlight.

Susan found it hard to remember what Aslan said. It was almost as if he had spoken inside her mind. It was so clear, so logical, so sensible. And

yet it was warm and loving, too.

Aslan asked where Edmund was, and Mr. Beaver explained that he had betrayed them to the White Witch.

"If this is true, then why does he deserve our help?" asked Aslan calmly.

"Because it's my fault, really. I was too hard on him," Peter said.

Susan felt proud of Peter; he had said something very difficult.

And she saw that it wasn't fair for Peter to take the blame on his own. "We all were," she said.

"Sir, he's our brother," Lucy added, which was what they all felt and hadn't said. And suddenly, Susan knew Aslan would find Edmund. Everything was going to be all right.

Afterward, Susan and Lucy washed their hair and tried on a pile of Narnian silks. They were so beautiful. Green, blue, silver, opal—Susan couldn't believe the soft shining fabric that slid through her fingers like gossamer. Then they ran down to the stream to see how they looked in their new finery.

"Mum hasn't had a dress like this since before the War," said Susan, admiring her reflection in the water.

Lucy had an idea, "We should bring her one when we go back. A whole trunk full!"

Susan saw Lucy's face and felt guilty. "*If* we ever get back . . . I'm sorry I'm like that," she said. "We used to have fun together, didn't we?"

"Yes! But that's before you got boring." Lucy smiled and she flicked a handful of water at her sister. Susan grinned and splashed back. Soon they were playing happily in the stream, screaming with laughter.

But two pairs of yellow eyes were watching them coldly. They belonged to the White Witch's Wolves, Maugrim and Vardan. With a low snarl, the bigger Wolf loped out of hiding.

Susan whirled around.

"Please don't run," said Vardan viciously as Maugrim dropped down beside him. "We're tired and we'd prefer to kill you quickly."

Susan was terrified. Her hand went to her pocket—but the horn that Father Christmas had given her was not there! Of course—it was in her old skirt. She nodded very slightly at Lucy, who snatched up a handful of gravel from the stream and threw it in Maugrim's face. He staggered back, and Susan ran like mad toward her clothing. She could see the horn poking out of her pocket where she had left it.

Maugrim was almost on top of her. She could hear his hideous panting as she fumbled to get the horn to her lips. She blew with all her might. Immediately there was a mighty sound like a clarion of trumpets and as she paused in surprise, Lucy pulled her toward the nearest tree. The Wolves, too, hesitated vital seconds, shocked by the horn blast. The girls had scrambled up several branches before Maugrim was snapping uselessly at Susan's dangling robes.

At that moment, Peter arrived with Aslan and a band of Narnians, and Maugrim leapt toward him, snarling with delight. Then everything was

wild confusion. Susan saw Peter and Maugrim struggling on the ground, the Wolf growling horribly and lunging at Peter's neck. Lucy was screaming and Aslan had the other Wolf as a prisoner—but why wasn't Aslan helping her brother? He seemed to be keeping everyone away from the fight. With a ghastly groan, the huge Wolf shuddered and lay still, almost crushing Peter. The second Wolf, now miraculously free, leapt into the bushes and disappeared. It had all happened so fast that Susan had hardly had time to be scared.

Now Aslan was telling Peter to kneel. He was making Susan's brother a knight. Had the fight with Maugrim been some kind of test? Or had it been Aslan's way of helping her brother to discover the strength inside him, the strength he had not been able to find that last time on the ice?

It wasn't long before Susan worked out why Aslan had set the other Wolf free. She felt a pang

of admiration for his wisdom, because now a host of Narnians were hunting Vardan. The Wolf would run to the Witch and where the Witch was, they would also find Edmund.

The rest of the day and that night, Susan and Lucy waited impatiently for news of their brother. And at dawn the following day, Susan staggered sleepily out of her tent to see . . . Edmund, walking wearily into camp behind Aslan.

She checked herself and said, "Are you okay?" And then she couldn't hold back any longer and hugged him with all her strength. He was back! Now they could all go home and forget this nightmare that was Narnia. They would go back to being a normal family doing normal things, and there would be no killing or turning to stone, no talking animals or witches or wild spirits of any kind.

After breakfast, Peter revealed his plan for them all. He wanted to send Susan, Edmund and Lucy home. He had promised their mother he would keep them safe. But he was staying. Peter had promised Aslan that he would help in the battle against the White Witch.

"We can't leave now!" cried Lucy.

Susan agreed with Peter. They had all nearly

been killed, they had traveled day and night without food—what more could they do? It wasn't their war. She looked hopefully at Edmund. After what he had been through with the White Witch, surely he would support her.

But to Susan's amazement, Edmund wanted to stay. He told them how he had been beaten and starved by the White Witch, how he had seen her deceive creatures and trick them into giving themselves and their families away and then tortured them or turned them to stone.

"I've seen what the Witch can do. I helped her do it. I'm not leaving these people behind to suffer for it," he said.

Susan looked around at their resolute faces. She could see more clearly than her brothers and sister how close they had all come to being killed. She guessed they would come just as close—maybe closer—in the future. But Peter, Edmund and Lucy were right. There were times when you had to stand up against what you knew to be wrong.

"I guess that's it then," she said quietly.

"Where are you going?" asked Peter fearfully.

Susan took her new bow and arrows.

"To get in some practice."

But there was another far more terrible surprise waiting for Susan that morning. The

Witch had arrived to speak with Aslan. According to the ancient laws of Narnia, all traitors belonged to her. Unless the Witch had Edmund's blood as the law demanded, all Narnia would be destroyed.

Chapter Six

Loss and Triumph

Susan could not believe what she was hearing. Aslan had saved Edmund. How could he let the Witch triumph at the last moment? Aslan gave a rumbling growl like thunder and asked the Witch to talk with him in private. The Witch laughed and sneered, and it was clear that she thought she had won.

The next few hours were the hardest that Susan had spent in Narnia. There was nothing that anyone could say that could possibly make things better. Edmund sat silently on the ground, waiting to hear what was going to happen to him.

When Aslan reappeared with the Witch, the children jumped to their feet.

"She has renounced her claim on your brother's blood," said Aslan sadly.

The Narnians cheered wildly. Susan hugged Edmund tight, but she felt scared. What had Aslan promised? The Witch signaled to her servants to take her away.

Late that night, Susan woke suddenly to find Lucy bending over her.

In a second, Susan was putting on her slippers, and the two girls slipped outside. They could see Aslan ahead of them, his golden mane like a halo of fire. All of a sudden, he turned and

Susan longed to hug him, but she did not dare. He looked sadder than they had ever seen him.

"Please, couldn't we come with you?" she pleaded.

Aslan paused as if he was considering. "I'd be

glad for the company," he said as the girls came to his side, "but promise me you'll stop when I tell you."

And in perfect silence the three walked across the empty plain, with no sound but the beating of their hearts and their soft footsteps on the ground. They climbed the steep slope toward the Stone Table, and then Aslan gave them one last sad look and told them to return.

"And no matter what," he warned, "do not let yourselves be seen by anyone!"

Unable to leave the spot, the girls wriggled closer to the hilltop, which was now lit with torches. Susan watched Aslan walk steadily up to the Stone Table, where the Witch was waiting for him, surrounded by a host of hopping, shrieking, snarling, creeping things too hideous and evil to bear the light of day. Tossing back her wild hair in the torchlight, she was radiating a kind of terrible ecstasy.

"Bind him!" she screamed. At first the creatures were scared, but when Aslan made no effort to defend himself, they rushed at him, yelping and screeching.

Susan gasped. Why didn't he stop them? She grabbed hold of Lucy in case she ran out to help. There was nothing they could do.

The creatures tied Aslan's paws together and dragged him on to the Stone Table. Then they mocked him and shaved off his glorious golden mane. It was too much to take. Susan rocked back and forth in pain and misery, and Lucy wept openly.

But the hideous ceremony was rising to a climax. The Witch pulled back her sleeve and raised her deathly white hands.

She jeered, "Did you honestly think that by all this you would save the Human traitor? You have given me your life and saved no one's. Tonight

the Deep Magic will be appeased, but tomorrow we will take Narnia back . . . forever. In that knowledge despair . . . and die!"

And she plunged a stone knife deep into Aslan's heart.

Susan and Lucy watched, terrified, as the Witch and her servants withdrew. The girls clung together, crying for the Great Lion.

But back at the Stone Table, something very strange was happening.

Lucy and Susan were not far from Aslan's body when there was a terrific rumbling, like an earthquake. The hill shook and they fell to the ground as a tremendous explosion seemed about to tear them apart. They stood up groggily and, to their amazement, the Stone Table had split in two and Aslan had disappeared.

"Is this more magic?" whispered Susan, awed.

"Yes. It is more magic." And there, more

glorious than ever, his mane shining in the first rays of the rising sun, was Aslan.

"But we saw the knife! The Witch—!" cried Susan, bewildered.

Aslan explained that the White Witch knew only of the Deep Magic, which had been created at the dawn of time, but that there was an older magic still, of which she knew nothing. This magic, created before the dawn of time, was founded on Good and Evil. And even the White Witch was no match for it.

"Susan, Lucy, we have work to do," said Aslan.

Nothing could have prepared the girls for the wonder of climbing on Aslan's back and racing like the wind across plains, through woods and over hills. Their breath was whipped out of their mouths and they hardly spoke until Susan began to recognize the landscape. She saw the Beavers' dam and the river, and the twin hills by the Witch's castle. Aslan scarcely paused at the gates, but leapt over the wall in one huge bound. There stood the sad and fearful statues of Narnians turned to stone by the Witch. Susan was horrified. To think that she had almost helped this evil Witch who had murdered so many innocent creatures. . . .

Aslan bent over a Faun and breathed on him.

"Lucy Pevensie!" cried Mr. Tumnus.

"Susan, this is Mr. Tumnus," Lucy introduced

her friend, the Faun, to her sister.

"Mr. Tumnus!" Susan smiled, hugging the Faun as he miraculously came back to life. Soon there was a host of bewildered and happy Narnians in the courtyard, talking and laughing and preparing to march back to fight on the Narnian side.

"Peter will need reinforcements," said Aslan. "And we may already be too late!"

The battle was going against the Narnians, but when the Witch's army saw Aslan they howled in terror and the reinforcements joined in with a joyful cry. Susan scanned the battlefield anxiously. Where were her brothers? Her heart almost stopped. There was Peter, exhausted, and Edmund was lying wounded on the ground. And a menacing Dwarf was lifting up his axe to kill him! Cool as ice, Susan plucked an arrow from her quiver and aimed at the Dwarf. The arrow's metal tip pieced the Dwarf's shoulder and he

sank to the ground with a groan. "Edmund!" she shrieked.

Peter, Susan and Lucy raced to Edmund's side, and with a drop of the magical liquid given to her by Father Christmas, Lucy healed Edmund's wounds.

As Father Christmas had said, battles are ugly,

and part of Susan was glad that they had not arrived sooner. She and Lucy hurried from wounded Narnian to wounded Narnian, giving them drops of the life-giving fireflower juice. She was dimly aware of the victorious shouts of the Narnians. Aslan himself had dealt with the White Witch and now, without her to drive them on, only the departing howls of the Witch's army rang in Susan's ears.

The next days passed in a blur of activity. There was so much to clear up, so much to organize. Susan no longer thought of going home. She could only plan for what was about to happen. The four children were to be crowned at Cair Paravel, as Mr. Beaver had promised what seemed like years ago, at the start of their adventure.

And so, exactly as the prophecy had foretold, Susan found herself sitting on her throne, in a long silken gown, with a crown of golden flowers

on her head. She was now Queen Susan, the Gentle, and her past life was fading like a dream.

Some years later, four young Kings and Queens were riding through a wood on the very edge of Narnia. They had lost their way and evening was coming on. Suddenly Queen Susan spotted a strange iron tree with a lantern on top. It seemed oddly familiar. They dismounted, and through the trees they could faintly see an open door. The feeling of magic was very strong and before any of them quite realized what was happening, they had gone through that door.

Seconds later, four noisy children bounced out of a large old wardrobe. In front of them, the door of a room opened and a very curious Professor Kirke looked at the startled group.

Peter and Susan, Edmund and Lucy had been away perhaps half a second. Susan looked around at her sister and brothers. They had had adventures that nobody would believe, but she had done it. Susan had promised their mother she would keep the family together and she had. She smiled up at Professor Kirke.

EXCERPT FROM

Peter's Destiny: The Battle for Narnia

Adapted by Craig Graham

CHAPTER ONE

At the Professor's House

Peter Pevensie tried his best to look interested.

"Come on, Peter," said Susan, his sister. She was holding an open dictionary. "Gastrovascular."

"Is it Latin?" asked his brother, Edmund, stifling a yawn. "For 'worst game ever invented'?"

Susan shut the dictionary with a thump.

"We could play hide-and-seek," said Lucy, the youngest.

"But we're already having so much fun." Peter sighed.

"Hide-and-seek's for children," Edmund added.

Lucy jumped to her feet.

"Come on, Peter!" she cried. "Please?"

Peter sighed again, then covered his eyes.

"One, two, three, four . . ."

As he counted, Peter thought about how he and his brother and sisters had come to be here, miles from home and living with people they didn't even know. Air raids had made London a dangerous place, so many of the city's children were evacuated to the country. Peter's mother had taken them to the railway station with their luggage and boarded them onto a train.

"Promise me you'll look after the others," she had said to Peter, tears in her eyes.

"I will, Mum," he said, hugging her.

The house they were staying in belonged to Professor Kirke. It was a big, old mansion with stained glass windows. The Professor lived alone, except for his housekeeper, Mrs. Macready, so there was plenty of room for them all. They hadn't seen the Professor yet, as he was always working, but Mrs. Macready seemed a little grumpy. She had already warned them against shouting, running, sliding down the banisters and touching the Professor's things.

"Ninety-nine, one hundred. Ready or not, here I come!"

Peter opened his eyes. No one was in the room. He stepped out into the hall.

"It's all right!" cried Lucy, bursting out of a big wardrobe. "I'm back!"

Edmund stuck his head out from behind a curtain. "Shut up! He's coming."